a blaze in the BUSH

Written by Kat Lux

Illustrated by Raf Luyckx

Printed in Australia
Cover design by Shawline Publishing Group Pty Ltd
Illustrations within this book © Raf Luyckx

First Printing: August 2023
Shawline Publishing Group Pty Ltd
www.shawlinepublishing.com.au
Paperback ISBN 978-1-9228-5160-4
Ebook ISBN 978-1-9228-5165-9

PLAYTIME BOOKS

A catalogue record for this work is available from the National Library of Australia

DISCOVER MORE OF OUR NEW TITLES

With this book I would like to acknowledge the silent heroes that inspired me to create a story about sacrifices made and risks taken by real people: The RFS (Rural Fire Service) and every fire fighter (professional or volunteer); Toni Doherty (whose video went viral after selflessly rescuing a burnt koala from the Lindfield Park Road bush fire in 2019); Ellenborough Lewis, the koala from beforementioned video (who was treated at Port Macquarie Koala Hospital after the event) and all of Australia's wildlife suffering from injuries or habitat loss after bush fires; Julie Fletcher (who sadly passed away in a bush fire in the Mid-Coast region in 2019) and all bushfire victims nationwide; Sue Ashton (president), Cheyne Flanagan (clinical director) and all the staff and volunteers of the Port Macquarie Koala Hospital.

Somewhere in the Eucalypt Forest a stuffy smoke filled the steaming hot air. Fast flames skipped from one tree to another. Everything in between sizzled and snapped.

Fletch the koala shook some ashes from his ears. 'Has it ever been so bad, Lewie?'

'Every year things are getting worse,' Lewie the kangaroo replied. 'Those fires start because it's too dry. I wish we would get some rain, the dust stings in my eyes.'

Fletch started thinking. 'You can't start a fire without a spark. So that is what we have to look for.'

'It's tricky to look for a spark. A spark is over in an instant, as fast as a sneeze from a stuffy nose. It's what follows the spark that lingers on,' Lewie said wisely.

Tonia was a girl who lived at the brink of the forest. Every day she would bring some water for the animals. Today, Tonia held a scarf in front of her face and left very quickly. The breeze had brought traces of the fire smell that masked the eucalypt scent.

Eagerly, Lewie took a mouthful of water while Fletch climbed down from his tree for a sip. How refreshing! They would have liked to wash the dust from their faces also, but knew they were not the only thirsty creatures in the forest.

The next day, Fletch saw a new plume of smoke rising on the other side of the forest. With no rain cloud in sight, he decided to call a meeting. Dawn the kookaburra lent a hand with spreading the word.

There was only one topic to be discussed, one that everyone could sniff... I mean guess.

Fletch spoke about his fear. 'We do not know where or how the blazes start, but if we don't find out soon, our forest will not survive.'

'I think I know something,' Ned the frogmouth whispered cautiously. 'People make fire for fun.'

'People bring us water when the creeks have dried up,' Lewie replied.

Cheyne the possum added, 'We can only know something for sure when we see it with our own eyes.'

That is how the *'Wood Watch Team'* was formed. Everyone was tasked with patrolling a part of the forest. Cheyne and Ned took on the night shift while Dawn signed up to keep an eye on the people right outside the woodland. They each took some water and went their own way to protect their home.

Dawn saw that the people didn't make fire for fun, like Ned said. On the contrary, they tried to fight it with all they had available, which did not look like enough for such a blaze.

‘Haaa-choo... OH NO!’

Fletch heard a sneeze, followed by a sob. He saw a little dragon stamping out the little sparks that came out after every sneeze.

‘Haaa-choo!’ the little dragon went again. This time the spark was too quick and it turned into a little flame. Fletch came running and put it out with some water from his bottle. Phew! Only just in time.

Ash the little dragon whimpered, ‘It always goes like that. My nose gets prickly and then I sneeze. I just can’t help it.’

Fletch tried really hard to put out every little spark,
but there were too many and they spread too quickly.
The wind was strong and made the sparks spread further.

Meanwhile, Ash kept sobbing that it was all her fault, but she couldn't stop the sneezing. 'Come with me,' Fletch said and he pulled Ash to Cheyne's tree.

Cheyne prepared a mixture for stuffy noses of sneezing dragons. She mixed some eucalyptus oil with the last little bit of water in Fletch's bottle.

'Haaa, haaa, haaa–' Cheyne ducked away, just in time for the risky '–choo!'

As fast as he could, Fletch held his finger under Ash's nose and Cheyne quickly came forward to let her smell the mixture. Ash stopped sneezing. Cheyne poured the remainder of the mixture in a bottle, laced it on a piece of rope and placed it around Ash's neck.

In the meantime, the fire raged on. The friends of the forest had nothing left to do besides seek shelter for the disaster that would come. Ash flapped away with cheerless wing-strokes and with great sadness she looked back at what she left behind. Fletch climbed high into the treetops, the birds left their nests and flew towards safety. The other animals sought cover in their burrows, holes or hideaways.

The fire raged for days on end until everything turned black and nothing was left to feed the flames.

It was late in the afternoon when Fletch heard the flapping, followed by wailing calls. He looked up and with eyes that stung and ears that rung, he saw Ash drawing near. Behind Ash followed the rain bringers – cockatoos, as black as the branches beneath them. Ash landed in a tree beside Fletch and said, 'The rain is coming; it's over.' Fletch peered down and could only hope that it wouldn't be too late for his friends down there.

The sky started to drip... to rain... to pour...

The grey clouds above emptied for days on end. The ground was covered with broken branches and tarry black puddles formed in the once so green Eucalypt Forest.

The friends of the forest found each other again after the rain. They jumped and splattered in puddles. The relief was felt in the frisky mood that the sun had brought. But someone was missing... Lewie was nowhere to be seen.

Lewie's burrow hadn't been spared. It made Fletch very sad to find his best mate like this and he had to swallow away his salty tears. The bush fire was a brutal enemy.

The animals of the Eucalypt Forest said their last goodbye to their friend. Ash watched from a distance and a tear fell to the ground. Nobody knew back then that dragon tears had magic in them. With these magical teardrops, Ash made the soil fertile where she had unwillingly caused such destruction before. Fresh green sprouts shot up and made this sad day a little more bearable.

That is how, each time there was a bush fire after that day, Ash thought of what had happened to Lewie and once again her magical tears would roll down to the earth, helping new life grow.

PLAYTIME BOOKS

Milton Keynes UK
Ingram Content Group UK Ltd.
UKRC031046190923
428966UK00002B/9

9781922851604